All these years science fiction
has been getting us ready
for the world we live in now.
~ *(pg. 20)*

Also by Mary Lee Bragg

2

Shooting Angels (2004)

How Women Work (2010)

Winter Music (2012)

The Landscape That Isn't There (2019)

Airplane Earth

Mary Lee Bragg

720 – Sixth Street, Box # 5
New Westminster, BC
V3C 3C5   CANADA

Title: Airplane Earth
Author: Mary Lee Bragg
Publisher: Silver Bow Publishing
Cover Art: "Evidarian Nadir" painting by Candice James
Layout/Design/Editing: Candice James
ISBN: 978-1-77403- 295-4 paperback
ISBN: 978-1-77403- 296-1 e- book

Library and Archives Canada Cataloguing in Publication

Title: Airplane Earth / Mary Lee Bragg.
Names: Bragg, Mary Lee, author.
Description: Poems.
Identifiers: Canadiana (print) 20240317009 | Canadiana (ebook) 20240317017 | ISBN 9781774032954
   (softcover) | ISBN 9781774032961 (Kindle)
Subjects: LCGFT: Poetry.
Classification: LCC PS8603.R334 A75 2024 | DDC C811/.6—dc23

**To Colin
who makes it happen**

6

Table of Contents

Mary Writes a Letter to Rachel

The envelope is addressed to Mrs. Norman Bragg,
c/o General Hospital and four cents postage brought it
from Rockyford to Calgary in time to reach her there.
Another hand has pencilled *Maternity* above the name.
It is date stamped the day after my birthday
and on the back are pencil tracings of a baby's hand and foot.

Grandma speaks of *great rejoicing*.
Without seeing me, she is sure I am *a lovely daughter*.
The neighbours are having girls too.
       Everyone gets what they want.
One has named his baby Lauretta Ann,
and she cautions *Don't you pick a name like that.*

She has canned 15 quarts of cherries for the family,
and 15 pints for Dad. (He would not live to eat them,
those sugarless diabetic cherries.)
Grandchildren are swimming in the irrigation ditch,
and *everyone is happy*.
She calls my mother *darling girl* and signs off,
       Good times are ahead.

Grandma includes another note, from her daughter Mary,
who is also busy canning 23 pints of rhubarb.

My aunt's spelling is ad lib
(the second "E" in Henry and the "K" in picnic)
but she conveys *hemorrhagic septicemia*
clear enough.
Her husband is vaccinating calves.

This is what my mother read in *Maternity*
in that week before our lives together began.
She traced my hand and foot
and put the envelope in her scrapbook.
She wanted me to be like them,

to preserve the sweetness of that moment,
so, she named me Mary.

Then,
because she was my mother,
because cautioning about a *name like that*
is like saying *Don't think about alligators*,
        she made it Mary Lee.

Voices in the Dark

My brother phones me.
I phone my sister.
I phone her daughter.

*She's actively dying,
if that oxymoron isn't too weird.*

I phone another niece.
I phone my sister again.
I phone another brother.

Sometimes we lapse into silence
that we break together, saying
Well, anyway . . .

We could do this another way.
Zoom or Facetime,
things we do with other people.

For this
we are back
to listening in the dark.

As we listened to the radio
when we were kids,
blankets pulled to our chins.

This Long Dying

I am watching fur hats and MAGA caps
invade the US Capitol when
my brother calls with the news.

It's hard to see your sister die,
your elder and idol,
the one who smoked and danced
and grew up too fast.

I talk to her children.
'Hallucinating' they say.
She who never drank
or did drugs eased out of life
on a tidal wave of opiates.

This long dying sapped us all.
Covid to Christmas
and crisis after crisis it went on.

One niece mourns a son
dead by his own hand,
pauses in our talk to take her meds.
Another is helping a daughter
leave an unhappy man;
she sits among boxes to talk to me.

No funeral allowed.
Our days lengthen
toward inauguration,
hope still alive for that other sister,
the country our ancestors left,
the one assaulted
by her ungrateful children.

Out of Frame

The camera chooses what to see –
lectern, baptismal font and pulpit,
urn, ashes, photograph.

It does not pan out to show
the painting above the altar –
Christ in Gethsemane,
nadir of despair and doubt.
The picture I studied every Sunday.

We also choose how to see and say.

My sister lived eighty years
in the same small town,
kept friends from childhood to old age,
devoted to her children.

Out of frame
the fact that I spent my life
not living that one.

Sail Away

Oh, the years –
how many have passed since I read to my nieces,
their faces bright over the page, stories of horses
and the brave little girls who ride them,
Misty of Chincoteague and *Black Beauty.*

Now Sharon and I are the same age --
what difference does eight years make
in all our decades?
Her sister says she is in long-term care.

> *We had to take the place,*
> *the only one available.*
> *Fortunately, she doesn't seem*
> *to know where she is.*

She knows where she wants to go --
back to Narnia, where she will shoulder
a quiver full of arrows, keep her bowstring taut,
challenge winter and sail home to her kingdom.

Her friend will help her,
the red-headed kid whose name
she can't remember,
the orphan everybody picks on.

If she could stand,
Sharon would push into the closet,
past the winter coats,
dive into the smell of moth balls,
find a pony, a sailing ship,
a green-gabled house.

Lutherans Celebrate Easter

It starts Good Friday, with a service *Tenebrae*.
A reading and a hymn at each station of the cross,
then a drape drawn up, the image covered,
and lights turned down.

Fewer of us singing at each stop.

Finally, the spotlight's on the cross above the altar.
Two basses and a tenor sing the hymn,
'O Sacred Head Now Wounded'.
Cloth rises over the cross
and all the lights are doused.
Choir and congregants file out in silence.

Saturday ... Hornbachers is sold out of ham
and the bakery is pandemonium.
One of the altos says she'll cook a goose
and a couple of the tenors plan for turkey.

Sunday morning we're in the choir loft before dawn.
Someone struggled kettle drums up those stairs.
They've brought in a soprano from St. Paul
and three trumpeters stand beside the organ keyboard.
The church is silent as it was on Friday.

Light glows near the stained-glass window.
The drums rumble slow,
build until the trumpets blare,
the organ blasts,
the curtain drops from the altar cross,
and the choir exults
'Christ the Lord is Risen Today'.

The achingly beautiful voice
of the soloist from Saint Paul
soars above the congregation,

as if Mary Magdelene herself
had wafted over the fields
of soybeans and corn
to bring us
the good news.

Credo

The archangel Mormon wrote his gospel
on sheets of gold and buried it in upstate New York
for Joseph Smith to find.

The angel Gabriel dictated the Koran
to Mohammed.
God gave Moses the Law on tablets of stone
on Mount Sinai.

Valkyries take fallen warriors from the battlefield
to Valhalla on their winged horses.

Jesus Christ rose from the dead
on the third day.

Mohammed ascended into heaven
from the Dome of the Rock.

Lord Shiva is dancing, and when his foot
descends, the world will end.

The apocalypse will begin
when the seventh seal is opened.

Götterdammerung or Ragnarok,
the twilight of the gods is definite
as a black hole or an eclipse.

Finally, something I can believe.
Not Eden, but ending, feels right.
And I believe that the survivors
will light their cooking fires
with the pages of those books
and tell each other stories.

Even the Unbeliever

Even the unbeliever must believe
in something,
gravity, for example.

Even if you don't believe
it all happens according to laws
that can be observed and expressed
in equations of stunning elegance –
even the sourest of cynics
has to admit it works.

You don't have to understand
or believe the equations;
just note the absence of Velcro.

We're not Velcro-ed to the earth.
We're grounded by gravity.
          Without it
we'd be north of Betelgeuse
if we ever hopped or skipped.

Birds swim in an ocean of air
which wouldn't be there without gravity.

All the stardust we're made of
would float free,
anonymous atoms
without any opinions at all.

Maybe we could start with that.

Maybe we could all agree
we believe that gravity exists.

The Deaf Do Not Believe in Silence*
*** The deaf don't believe in silence. It is the creation of the hearing. ~ Ilya Kaminsky, *Deaf Republic* (endnote) 2019**

Fish do not believe in water.
Belief is not needed.

Throw yourself in
and the silent water
holds you up.

When you dance in moonlight
you don't have to notice
that your footsteps weave a quadrille
intricate as cobwebs
in the grass.

You don't have to believe
that all light is reflected,
    that probably none of this is real
    that certainly none of it matters.

      You only need to dance!

It's Fiction

All these years science fiction
has been getting us ready
for the world we live in now.

The commanders of Gilead
occupy the citadel;
they're burning books.

We're probing Jupiter
and robots talk
about their feelings.

It's not post-apocalyptic.
The disaster
isn't finished happening yet.

Our glasses will shatter
on the steps
of the ruined library.

The statue of a hand
holding a torch
will loom out of the sand.

Divination

By the stars,
by birds in flight,
by the entrails of sacrifice.

By tea leaves,
by a glove or photo,
Tarot spread or crystals
we seek to know the future.

Who will survive?
Who will thrive?
Where will the money come from?

We think so little of the past.
And yet it tells us all we need to know.

Hector's blood will spill out on the plain.
A baby will shatter below the battlements.
Helen will turn her back upon the burning city,
        and sail again to Sparta.

Laurels

It's that split second
when Apollo's hand grasps
her waist and she calls *'Father!'*
and father cannot blast a god,
but can encase his daughter in a sheath of bark.
Her upraised hands are growing leaves
and from her long toes, roots elongate.

Apollo is appalled.
His astonished face
and shrinking cock confirm
he wasn't expecting *this*.

But what about Daphne?
Did anyone ask her if she wanted
to be a tree, forever part of Apollo,
her leaves eternally crowning
the victors in his contests?

Would she rather have risked
the rough tumble with Apollo,
quick thrust, shame and confusion,
for the ability to walk away?

There are many ways
to transfigure and transform,
and father doesn't always know the best.

What poem would she have written,
and would we have crowned her
                    ... with laurels?

At the British Museum

When it rains, they pour
through the museum doors.

Crowds admire all this
archaeology – treasure buried
when the invaders were near,
helmets and swords from Saxon graves.

We pause before Parthenon
marbles, stand behind the masses
at the Rosetta Stone
grab selfies by Assyrian gates.

Too tired to talk about plunder
we find one place in perfect peace –
the Hall of Islamic Art.
Alone, we look at tiles and carpets,
trace curving cursive letters.

Crusaders admired these designs
and brought home cloth embroidered
with Arabic words.

Renaissance painters
wrapped them round
the Virgin Mary.

In oils today we see Virgin and Child,
bordered by

Allahu Akbar.
Allahu Akbar.
Allahu Akbar.

The Next New Thing

In their exhibit at the Glenbow,
the Nitsitapi tell us it was 1700
when they first saw
the animal called *ponoka omitaa* –
elk dog.

Big as an elk,
it pulled and carried
like a dog.

When Lewis and Clark met them
one hundred years later
the horse was more than dog or elk.
It was riches and war, buffalo hunt
and bride price.

One hundred years ago
horse power was everything.
Ploughs or carriages,
nothing moved without
a Clydesdale or a pony.

The new thing was *auto*
       mobile –
it moves itself.

We thought
it would make us free.

Flood Plain

The elevator at the apartment in the Marais
is too small for us and our suitcases,
so I ride up with the baggage
while my husband takes the stairs.

The room has a bed in one corner
and a TV at its foot,
stove and sink behind a counter,
bathroom tucked behind that.

The owners left a sliver of soap
in the shower,
a damp rag
in the sink.

On the tiny TV, flood waters
are spreading across Calgary,
the part everyone used to call the flood plain,
and the subtitled mayor of my old hometown
                    is saying
Do NOT canoe on the river NOW are you CRAZY?

But Paris is waiting.

We want to go out
and plot a foot path to the Louvre,
through the flood plain of the Seine.

We walk with GPS on a tablet
but no paper map, and each time
I touch our route the image jumps.

Good Old Days

These are the good old days.
I sleep as long as I want
and get up when I'm rested.

We have food in our cupboards and freezer
            and complain
because we have to clean the kitchen
          three times a day.

Clean water, hot and cold, runs from our taps
and we have electricity, cable and internet.

I have a device
that holds all the knowledge of the world.
I carry it in my hand
and don't like to be without it.

It is the sixth month of pandemic lockdown,
and we cope with jigsaw puzzles,
a new Netflix line up, novels,
and all the knowledge of the world
in our hands.

My husband hears me play,
          every day,
five of Satie's *Gnossiennes*,
and thinks he could too,
relearn the accordion lessons
of his youth.

With songbooks and earphones
he rattles the keys
of my electronic keyboard.
He rumbles *'The words of the prophets
are written on the subway walls'*.

The mightiest armies ever
are commanded by a madman.

It is before the election
and these are the good old days.

To My Television

You are rectangularly calm
in your place above the hearth.
From across the room, I summon you.
Tell me what is in the world.

You show me disaster after tragedy:
houses tossed in floodwaters,
cell phones' shaky pixels
blurred by atomized cement.

Your colour is true,
your sound fidelity itself.
You teach me to cook,
but not how to shop for those ingredients.

      You lead me into jeopardy
      but offer walk-in baths
      and stair chairs.

Late at night in your upper channels
the call of love resounds.
Its bouncing simulacrum warms the room
as once the fireplace did.

The Suitcases

They are puzzled, and dusty
from sitting so long on the shelf.

Now they are on the bed,
bewildered, empty,
or chaotically crammed
with things I do not need.

A pottery butter dish,
with butter,
wrapped in plastic,
is wedged among sock rolls.

The empty suitcase tempts me.
        I climb in,
breathe its cavernous air,
        stand on tiptoe,
reach as high as I can reach,
        and zip it shut.

Gnossiennes, Day 487 or so

Sixteen months in,
we're watching the 2020 Olympics,
as if the Year that Never Happened
can't stop coming back,
as if Time was Patient Zero.

In March, when we arrived home
as our leaders asked, I announced
       I will play these pieces every day
         until the pandemic ends.

Then I'd only learned three
of Satie's *Gnossiennes*,
and thought I'd have to struggle to learn
another two in time.

Five hundred repetitions later
this dreamy aimless music –
no key signatures or bar lines --
trickles from my fingers like honey.

I missed only one day --
       my second vaccine.

I wonder if I could quit this self-imposed discipline.
Then see the picture, the guy in a T shirt bragging
     'Unmasked Unvaxxed Unafraid'
and know this could last forever.

I bend over the piano, reach five octaves,
as if I'm embracing the keyboard,
run my fingers
      so exactly
through those chromatic runs
     and in all this time,
     all those rehearsals,

500 repetitions,
give or take,

31

I haven't managed
to memorize the *Glossiness*.

Even without a time signature
I still count under my breath.

Wall Guy *

The classical musician
survives the war in Warsaw
because art lovers hide him
and sometimes give him food.

In an empty apartment
he must remain completely silent
but hears people next door
play with the piano.

The woman slashes her way through
a classic for easy (and untuned) piano.

Her partner growls *Liebchen!*
and sweeps her off the bench
for grunting, slappy sex
right there on the floor.

I think of the guy
on the other side of the wall
whenever I approach my own piano.

I will him to unclench his fists,
relax his grip on that handful of hair,
and subside into a chair.

I play Reveries, Traumeries, Adagios
            for Wall Guy.
Lullabies and ballads
trickle from my fingers to his nerves.

From the other side of the wall,
a violin sobs
        something Slavic,
        Bartok or Dvorak.

I think it is Natalya,
who came to meet us
when she moved next door.

She is a doctor,
working in public health.

Not long ago, when this all began,
the people of our city
came out of our houses at 7 pm
and made noise for her and her friends.

See The Pianist, a film by Roman Polanski*
**** not during pandemic lockdown**

Fever Dreams
by Zostavax™

You are hot, so your hips move
and you moan, though you don't see
who touches you. Your legs
are slick with sweat.

You are in a plane, with fire
between you and the cockpit.

The pilots swear in German,
which you understand.

The plane lurches and tosses, jarring
you against window and armrest.

Someone calls
Marly, Marly, it's all right,
and you wake.

You don't know this sprite,
with her hair in elf-locks
and her wide anxious eyes,
nor why she mispronounces your name.

You tell her about the vivid movie
you just saw,
how the recorded explosions
shook the theatre seats.

You realize you are still asleep,
looking up at the glass ceiling
        of consciousness,
as if through deep water,
and you want to go there
but don't know how to swim
        or through what.

You awake, go to the bathroom,

drink water, put on dry pajamas,
and return to bed, where sleep
seizes you in its jaws
and rushes you to the edge
of a desert.

You hear the famous actor intone
I met a traveller in an antique land;

and you see how the lone and level sands
      stretch for you.

Subtext: Day 500 *or so*

We watched the Swedish movie,
the one about the marriage,
and the subtitles ran continuously,
even when the characters weren't speaking.

We didn't notice right away
that words and actions
were out of sync,
since that's what the movie
was really about.

But by the end, when the embrace at the door
      was subtitled
I always hated your smug oily smile
      and the welcome drink
Send an ambulance right away

By then we knew something was wrong.
But it was so right for that movie
and we were so stoned,
more merry than stunned,
that we watched the last half hour
      with no subtitles,
and understood everything,
as if the script was written for us.

We Are Occupied by Freedom
(*Ottawa, 2022*)

30/01
Our streets are clogged,
our vocabularies updated.
It's not *asshat* or *a-hole*.
It's *airhorn*.

A pied piper brought them to town.
In the Middle Ages people killed
the dogs and cats
that killed the rats.
Now they're anti-vax.
Freedom for some is prison for others.
I do not leave the house.

1/02
I wake to the sound of heavy machines.
First thought: armoured personnel carrier.
But no, it's just a snow plow.

7/02
The politicians debate:
is occupation a federal, provincial
or municipal responsibility?

9/02
The honkening continues.
Driving makes me nervous:
which laws will that truck obey?

18/02
Switch channels
between figure skating
and police action.
Perfect choreography.
No tasers or truncheons.
No flame throwers on the horses.

21/02
The bouncy castle is deflated.
The hot tub is drained.
Signs threatening the prime minister
with sexual violence are gone.

We clean up, count the cost.
Peace, trust, friendships broken.

We call it the *craziness*
as if a name could make it abnormal.

Les Quatre Chevaliers

Of course, they're not on horses.
Who does that anymore?

Pestilence rides a Harley –
a smoking, noisy hog –
and rears up, turning donuts
in the parking lot.

War rolls up in a convoy
of trucks and tanks,
soldiers under canvas
waiting their turn.

Famine walks barefoot.
Starving people cut
his horse to ribbons
and ate it raw.

And Death?
Death sees no reason
to park his sacral iliac
on a horse's bony back.

He lolls under a tree
while the other three work.
If he had lips, a cigarette
would dangle from them.

Death loves our villains,
and quotes our heroes.

Death needs ammunition
         not a ride.

Ukrainian Forces Retake Bucha

The map shows where they found the bodies.

Lyudmila, 54, on her doorstep.
Oleksandre, 25, in the street.
The mayor and her husband and their son,
with all their fingers broken,
at the school.

And in the commentary
these words appear.

Fake news
New York Times not a credible source

On the map no arrow points.
No sign says, 'You Are Here'.

Nameless naked woman in the basement
among the condom wrappers

Were you there?

Da Pravda.

Tallahassee Hot Yoga

The shooter travels from out of town,
consults schedules online, signs up
for the five pm he thinks will be busy.

He is looking for women –
women who wear yoga pants,
leave the house,
refuse to sleep with him.

They are in child's pose
when he opens fire and kills two.
Then, the only man in the class
attacks him
with an upright vacuum cleaner
and everyone else runs.

It's as if they set out, these two,
to show the extremes
of masculine behaviour,
even in their choice of tools.

The loser with the Luger,
the *incel* who labels himself
by what he doesn't do
and hasn't got.

And

The hero who wears tights but no cape,
and like some potent god,
hurls the vacuum
into him.

Molecules

White Supremacy is like high-fructose corn syrup.
It's in everything and it all tastes normal.

It's in the ketchup and the hot dog you put it on,
in the breakfast cereal and the orange juice
and glazed on the bacon.

It's in everything, and it thickens the blood,
clogs the arteries, slows the heart.
          But it's so sweet,
everything should taste like this,
all the time.

I listened to the hockey announcer
who couldn't pronounce Mahovlich or Cournoyer,
watched *Gone with the Wind* and sighed
          how elegant, how sad –
and the tunes for both shows
bring a tear to my eye
and the tear tastes sweet.

Drink a coke, or flavoured water.
Molecules slip the barrier, enter the blood
and become part of you.

You who could be
made of iron, and glow like phosphorus.

An Education

We were schooled in Palaces,
Capitol places – the Plaza, Rialto, Tivoli –
red-carpeted foyers lined with mirrors,
mirrors reflecting mirrors
and vistas of fronded plant.

We learned *How the West Was Won,*
the river *Kwai* was bridged,
the *Ten Commandments* handed down.

We learned that the correct response
to being slapped is *Thanks,*
I really needed that.

Much later, we learned
who wrote the script.

Acting Lessons

The actors who depict work on screen
are working; they are working at acting.

They make beds by flapping sheets
in billowing sails, not by heaving mattresses
and tucking hospital corners.

The woman ironing in the movies
is always pressing a white rectangle –
a pillowcase or tea towel – never
ferreting around a shirt collar
or the pintucks on a bodice.

The dish washer scours the cast iron frying pan
with steel wool, then drops it into a sink
full of suds, on top of the plates.

In the movies, two people play the piano –
a talking face above the keyboard
and anonymous hands
who do the actual playing.

The guy who put his face in mine
and sang *Chattanooga Choo-Choo*
while I was playing Scott Joplin's *Solace*
had obviously seen this movie.

Let's not talk about pornography.

A Gentleman

45

A gentleman Is always the hero,
impeccably tailored,
usually a tenor but sometimes
a solitary brooding baritone.

A gentleman may or may not dance,
depending on whether the author
is a man or a woman.

A gentleman does not offer you
a seat on the bus,
because a gentleman would not ride
a bus.

A gentleman does not run into a burning house
to rescue the children from an upstairs room,
but does reward the soldier
who emerges from the smoke
with a child under each arm.

A gentleman orders the infantry
to clear the protestors from the square,
and watches the work of boot and bayonet
from an upstairs window.

Heroes (Victorian)

Rochester has a wife in the attic
and a daughter in the schoolroom,
flirts with a guest in the gazebo,
schemes to elope with the governess,
and complains that he is lonely.

Darcy is rude and abrupt,
insults the heroine, disdains her family.
(She falls in love
when she sees his house.)

They'd make a lovely couple,
the Rochester-Darcys.

Darcy would lead Rochester
to the water, kneel to take off his boots,
remove his jacket,
tenderly unwind his cravat
for a dip in the fishpond.

In our age, they would marry,
and live at Pemberley, since
Thornfield Hall burned down.

The Darchesters would adopt
a covey of daughters:
one Jane who is plain,
one Jane who is beautiful,
one Jane who is bound to a scoundrel,
and doomed to be a sub-plot
in someone else's story.

Remember

Try to remember someone else's
most embarrassing moment.
You may recall a ruckus
in another corner of the room.

The guy in the bookstore in New York
whose voice carried from the front door
to the third floor where you browsed.
How dare you humiliate me like this!
I'm a lawyer! I'll sue!

Yes, you scrambled out of the pool
fast enough when the water turned green;
but do you remember whose legs
that cloud swirled around?

A sudden button on the dance floor
a breast saluting the music
sent you to the bathroom
to check the safety pins
in your own underwear.

So, go ahead. Eat the peach.
Let the juice run down your chin.
No one will notice, and if they do
they'll wish they had one too.

I Revise

Memory is a snapshot, not a movie.
You remember one scene, one line,
but not the conversation or the action
          before   or   after.

My aunt and uncle held their four-year-old
          upside down in our kitchen;
my uncle yelling,
          'He's choking to death!'

I don't remember what food or toy
Lyle had inhaled, or what it looked like
when they thumped it out of him,
but I recall the scene with an editorial sneer.

He's choking,
my nine-year-old self amended.
          It's only *to death*
          if he actually dies.

Parnassus

I will not summit Mount Poetry.

Nor will I be an anxious, ambitious corpse,
clutching an empty oxygen canister,
meters from the peak.

I'm enjoying this hike around the foothills.

That's me at base camp, feet on a log,
sipping tea from a tin mug,
trying to keep my bum warm
in a saggy canvas chair.

From the foothills, with binoculars,
you can see the earth curve,
telephone poles going over the horizon
like caravels sailing pennant first
        into Cabo da Roca.

Here comes someone down from the mountain
on the shoulders of the crowd, surprised,
a little stunned. The eager ones are poets,
not porters, and stagger under her weight.

I could help them hoist her up,
see her safe on the stony path to the village.
But here are bluebells hidden in the grass.
        Here is grass.

The Evolution of Dreams

50

Lost baby, car in the water,
    naked in public,
writing the exam for a class
    she's never been to –
at night she is a fraud or waif.

In retirement, she dreams
the creep of pantyhose,
shoulder pads in blouse and jacket,
        big hair.

Swelling like a puffer fish
at night she crosses lobbies,
        coffee in hand.

We Talk and Talk
***In Buddhism, the body is called a 'burning house'.
We talk and talk while our life burns away.***

I know this house
where flames lick at walls
and bookshelves while I saunter
from room to room,
gathering what I will need:
long strips of cloth,
a single earring.

Last night in this house
the staircases squeezed
to impassible tracks,
balconies overhung crevasses.

I have wandered its basements,
delivered by elevators
I can no longer find.
The man who accompanies me
is shrinking.

Once he stood waist high,
but now he's the size of a potato,
and his mouth has come loose
and hangs by a single peg.

We are alone in a parking garage
where all the cars are facing out.
All their lights come on at once.
The engines in the empty cars
growl to life, and they drive
at my potato man.

I step aside.

Island

You set a heading for the island
and sail into the dark.

You must not approach in daylight
or the island may not be there when you arrive.
If it hears an approaching motor
it may slip its coral collar
and slide into the rip current
that roars through the strait.

If you do land,
just as dawn tints the sky orange,
the sand will flinch under your feet
and you will stumble on the beach.

When you plunge your hands into the sand
remember to spread your fingers,
draw them gently toward you.

The island will understand
you are caressing it;
and will calmly allow you
to visit its beauties.

As you step toward the jungle,
a path will open.
Vines will frame
the entrance like columns,

Small red birds display themselves
on branches at eye level.

A lily swans toward you,
holding its chalice aloft.
Pale orchids crowd the forest path,
candles along the aisle.

Other People's Houses

We are good guests – smoke on the deck,
not in the kitchen, so we are out there
when the Wolf Moon
slides into eclipse and crowds
gathered at the beach begin to howl.

These kitchens are full of tools
I don't use – spurtle and coffee maker
with four pages of instruction.
No food of mine will ever need a mallet to subdue it.
Capers and lime marmalade in the fridge –
how will I nourish myself without the jumbo pack
of elbow macaroni and wedge of orange cheddar?

At night we learn that Memory Foam™
remembers someone else.
My husband emits a pleasant warmth,
apneal pops tell me he's still alive.
I would slide over there but my pyjamas cling
to the flannelette sheets.

I subside into the mattress dip
and dream of mountains.

I encounter little children:
who speak a strange musical language
who lead me on winding forest paths
who open grubby hands to show me their treasure.

Desire Lines

In Beacon Hill Park across the street
daffodils dance in the breeze.
Into them wades a young woman
in a turquoise sarong.

A scene from Renoir –
the blocks of colour, her graceful bend
as she picks a dozen flowers
and steps on twenty more.

From the stoop I say nothing.
I have scolded my own child
for picking flowers in the park,
but she is not mine,
and neither are the flowers.

She saunters past, swinging her bouquet
upside down, yellow against blue.

Daffodils are invasive.
Bulbs brought from Europe
multiply in this sandy soil
and the flowers will bloom again.

Later I cross the Garry Oak meadow
from playground to street, and hear
People like you ruin every fucking thing in the world!
The guy who camps beside the public washroom
is yelling from the asphalt path.
Even from a distance I can see the spittle fly.

He doesn't see the track I'm on,
a hard-packed narrow groove through the grass.
Geographers call them *desire lines*,
these trails connecting places we want to go.

The Songhees and Esquimalt people
once came here to gather blue calla lilies,
which now push up among the daffodils.

They left graves, cairns, blue flowers,
        and lines of desire.

On the Fault Line

Everyone knows what to do.
Billboards advertise *Preparedness Kits*.
The city website tells us *when the shaking stops
walk or bicycle to higher ground.*
If you are already safe, shelter in place
and help the people from down the hill.

The website does not say
no city employees will be available.

Everyone knows whether their house
is built on solid rock or gravel,
which streets run where the swamp was drained,
but not where the water went.
Everyone has shaken a bottle of ketchup,
        seen solid liquify.

Everyone knows that water speeds up
where the channel narrows,
though not all have heard of Bernoulli.
We've all sloshed water out of the bathtub
        standing up too fast,
but might not call them seiche waves.

We eye the narrow channel
and tell each other
the Strait of Juan de Fuca
is on the right side of the island.

Everyone listens
for the long, last withdrawing roar.

Dream House

57

The house of our dreams
is made of plywood
and has no windows.

We did not notice this
when we bought it.
The house front is brick,
and coloured light plays
on the hall floor
through stained glass
above the door.

We saw the deck at the back,
looking out over a lake
surrounded by trees,
soapy scum washing its shore.

But now the trees are dying,
a storm looms over the lake,
and the former owners
lurk in stairwells,
scolding us
when we squeeze past them
carrying tarps.

Airplane Earth

Stowaways tumble from overhead bins
as our plane cants to vertical.

Oxygen masks dangle,
but no air flows and who can reach?

Two passengers cram every cheap seat
and those crouched in the aisles
bowl to the front.

The half-dozen in the washrooms
are fucking
while the crowd in the galley
has licked clean every tray.

In first class pods,
the few recline;
watch zombie movies
on their pull-out screens
while the plane speeds up.

The windows are full of mountain
and the pilot hammers
on the cockpit door.

Animals of the Apocalypse

the Horsemen ride us down
no survivors stumble
through irradiated landscapes
or the shallows
of lukewarm seas

they emerge

Great Danes stilt-walk
through kudzu and bindweed
where gerbils and guinea pigs cower
snack on Shar-Peis

a boa constrictor oozes
from its terrarium and slides
through heating ducts
in search of fainting goats

a monkey
sheds its sheepskin coat
stands up and reaches
for a club

Strata

The Anthropocene won't always be
      the top layer.

When it is in the middle, it will be
a calm stripe around the globe,
      asphalt-black.

The presence and quality of fossils
in the layers above and below
will be noted
by beings who care.

The Velociraptor Telescope

You tell me something is as useless
as a velociraptor telescope;
your point being that the raptor's eyes
were on the sides of its head.

But if a velociraptor built a telescope
it would make it for lizard eyes.

It would put its head inside,
and see above – Saturn before its rings –
and on the horizon
a comet flying low.

Climbing Uluru

We talk about eating meat –
whether we could save the world
if we stopped.

My friend believes
*One person's actions
don't make that much difference.*

Some fisheries will be exhausted
within ten years, meaning
we will have killed all the fish.
In that future pluperfect world
there will be no tuna, no cod.

*That's why I order fish
every chance I get.*

I change the subject, and mention
that no one can climb Ayer's Rock now,
Uluru restored to the people,
its song line undisturbed.

But when they announced the date,
people lined up to climb the rock.
Hundreds. More than ever.

*Of course, you'd want to climb
if you knew you couldn't do it next year.*

I have nothing to say.
I am eating sushi – ahi tuna
flown a thousand miles inland.

A Canadian Writes to a Future Generation

I'm sorry you live in the foreseeable apocalypse,
your feet burning on the sand
as you trek north in search of green.

I say this knowing
that if my predictions come true –
the world a dust bowl sloshed
by tepid seas full of plastic –
you probably can't read.
Maybe you're not even there.

But if you're reading this in the comfort
of your bubble on Mars
or the shade
of a genetically-engineered elm
            you may laugh.

People back then had an inflated
sense of their own importance.
They thought they were big enough
to kill a planet, as if they could ride
meteorites or surge through the mantle
like magma.

> *PS*
> Canada is a country on the northern half
> of the North American continent, which
> may be somewhere else by your time,
> or something else, but for now
> it's cold and clean.

> PPS
> (Cold = absence of heat
> Clean = you can breathe)

Acknowledgments

The following poems have been previously published:

The Four Horsemen in Bywords Quarterly, March 2022

Subtext League of Canadian Poets Poem of the Day

Heroes and *An Education* in *Laugh Lines*, an anthology by Repartee Press

At The British Museum, Bywords, October 2023

To My Television, in "Teasing the Tongue," (ed. Lorna Crozier), Wintergreen Studio Press, 2017

For their editorial assistance with this manuscript, I would like to thank Doris Fiszer, Susan Gillis, and Colin Morton.

For inspiration and encouragement to write it in the first place, thanks to members of the Ruby Tuesdays writing group: Susan Atkinson, Frances Boyle, Laurie Koensgen, Sneha Madhavan-Reese, Claudia Radmore, Lise Rochefort, Deborah-Anne Tunney, Jean Van Loon.

Special gratitude and fond memories of Jacqueline Bourque, a gem among rubies.

Author Profile:

Mary Lee Bragg lives in Ottawa with her husband, poet Colin Morton. Her poetry and short fiction have been published in *Ascent, Grain,* the *Windsor Review, Queen's Quarterly* and ezines in Canada and the US. She has published a novel, and two chapbooks of poetry. Her first full poetry collection, *The Landscape That Isn't There* (2019) was short-listed for Ottawa's Archibald Lampman prize.